TEACHER WORE PAJAMAS

Julie Christianson

Illustrated by Melissa Patrello

Abbott Press books may be ordered through booksellers or by contacting:

Abbott Press
1663 Liberty Drive
Bloomington, IN 47403
www.abbottpress.com
Phone: 1-866-697-5310

ISBN: 978-1-4582-1455-3 (sc)
ISBN: 978-1-4582-1454-6 (hc)
ISBN: 978-1-4582-1456-0 (e)

Library of Congress Control Number: 2014903217

Printed in the United States of America.

Abbott Press rev. date: 4/16/2014

abbott press®
A DIVISION OF WRITER'S DIGEST

For Alayna and Garrett, remembering all the bedtimes that began with "Tell me a story".

Thanks to all my supporters and believers. Ashley, you lead this list.

"Pajama Day Tomorrow" the school flyer read. She was a first year teacher and worry filled her head.

You see, about her PJs, well, there is a story there. She had worn them forever and they were her favorite pair.

Many years old and truth
be told, Teacher's jammies
were threadbare!

Her buttons on her top were wiggly.
The stitches were stretched loose.
But what would make the children giggly
is the bottoms... of her bottoms ...
were just about see-throughs!

The soft flannel fabric
was all faded. About that,
she did not care. But what
if, in Teacher's busy day, her
pajamas would rip or tear?

Oh goodness, she couldn't let that happen. The kids would see her underwear! Teacher started thinking that, for safety's sake, she had better pack a second pair.

Just about then Teacher's mom called as she knew she needed to. Moms have a way of knowing you need them, even before you do.

13

"What's your trouble dear?" Mom asked in her most concerned way. Mom smiled a little to herself when she heard about Pajama Day.

"The children will wear their Jammie Best," Mom told Teacher, "and you should do that too." Teacher agreed that she could wear her Christmas PJs. Those were still brand new.

That night Teacher's mom took the favorite pajamas home with her "for some TLC" she said. But Teacher's mom actually had a different plan going through her head.

While Teacher did her lesson plans Mom was busy sewing. Next morning she snuck into school without Teacher knowing.

Wearing all their Jammie Finest, Teacher and the children gathered there. At Circle Time they found a surprise waiting for them at Teacher's chair.

The chair was a rocker, made of wood and painted honey brown. But today it was regally dressed like a princess in a gown!

Flannel sleeves covered the arms of the chair. Soft, buttoned cushions lined the backrest and seat. And more very familiar looking fabric now ran down the chair's legs to its' feet.

You see, Mom had taken Teacher's favorite pajamas and used them to dress her rocking chair! When she realized what she was seeing Teacher was all smiles as she declared:

"Every time I sit here it will be as if my absolutely most favorite pajamas are wearing ME!"

And so Pajama Day went smoothly with Teacher wearing her Christmas pair. And what a relief to know she never ever worried about the kids seeing her underwear!

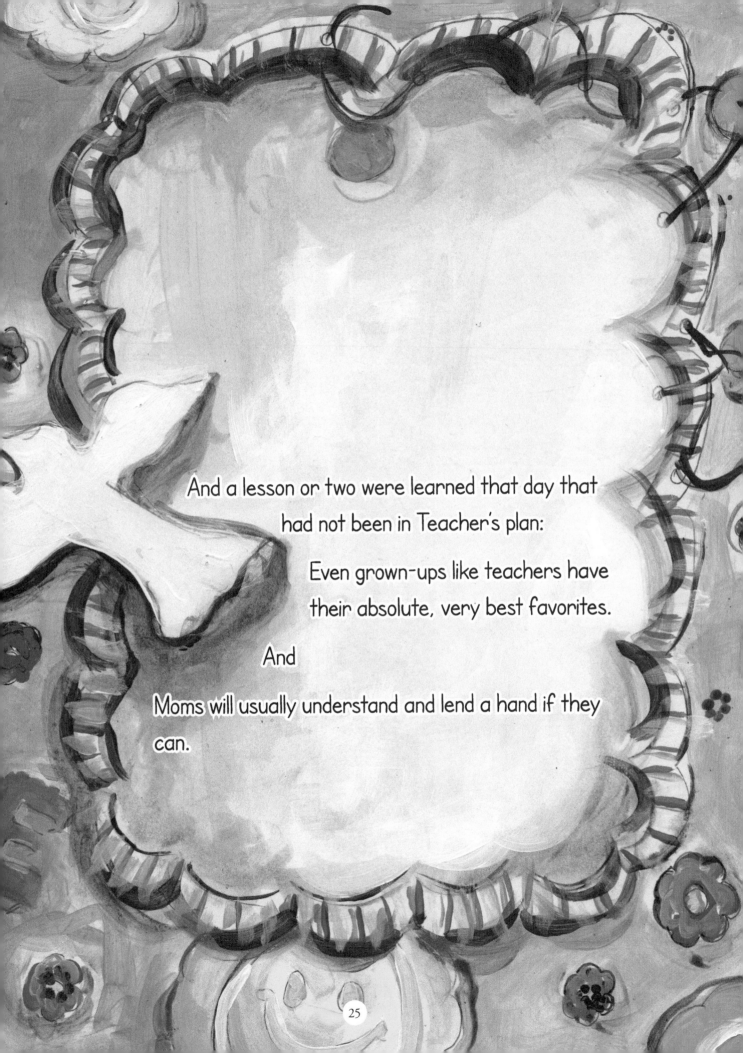

And a lesson or two were learned that day that
had not been in Teacher's plan:

Even grown-ups like teachers have
their absolute, very best favorites.

And

Moms will usually understand and lend a hand if they
can.

CPSIA information can be obtained at www.ICGtesting.com
Printed in the USA
LVOW02*0637300414

383819LV00004B/5/P